SCOOBY-DOO!
An Early Reading Adventure
SNOW MONSTER SCARE

By Robin Wasserman
Illustrated by Duendes del Sur

ABDOPUBLISHING.COM

Reinforced library bound edition published in 2017 by Spotlight, a division of ABDO. PO Box 398166, Minneapolis, Minnesota 55439. Spotlight produces high-quality reinforced library bound editions for schools and libraries. Published by agreement with Warner Bros. Entertainment Inc.

Printed in the United States of America, North Mankato, Minnesota.
042016   092016

THIS BOOK CONTAINS
RECYCLED MATERIALS

PUBLISHER'S CATALOGING IN PUBLICATION DATA

Names: Wasserman, Robin, author. I Duendes del Sur, illustrator.
Title: Scooby-Doo and the snow monster scare / by Robin Wasserman ; illustrated by Duendes del Sur.
Description: Minneapolis, MN : Spotlight, [2017] I Series: Scooby-Doo early reading adventures
Summary: Scooby and the gang are having fun playing in the snow and building a snowman. But after sledding, they discover that their snowman is missing his hat, scarf, nose and arms! It's a case only the Mystery Inc. gang can solve.
Identifiers: LCCN 2016930654 I ISBN 9781614794738 (lib. bdg.)
Subjects: LCSH: Scooby-Doo (Fictitious character)--Juvenile fiction. I Dogs--Juvenile fiction. I Snowmen--Juvenile fiction. I Snow--Juvenile fiction. I Mystery and detective stories--Juvenile fiction. I Adventure and adventurers--Juvenile fiction.
Classification: DDC [Fic]--dc23
LC record available at http://lccn.loc.gov/2016930654

Spotlight
A Division of ABDO
abdopublishing.com

Scooby and the gang were
playing in the snow.
They were building a snowman.
Velma made eyes out of buttons.
Daphne made a nose out of
a carrot.
Scooby made a mouth out of
Scooby-Snacks.

Fred made arms out of branches.
Shaggy finished dressing the
snowman with his hat and scarf.
"Like, this is the best snowman
ever!" said Shaggy.

Then Fred, Daphne and Velma
went down the mountain on
their skis.

Scooby and Shaggy followed on
a sled.

"Hang on!" said Shaggy.

"Scooby-Dooby-Doo!"
replied Scooby.

A while later, the gang went back to see their snowman. But something was wrong. The carrot, branches, hat and scarf—everything was gone! Scooby thought he smelled a carrot and started digging.

"Stop digging, Scooby," said Fred. "You're gonna cause an avalanche!"

Scooby continued digging.

"Will you stop for a Scooby-Snack?" asked Daphne. "We need to find our missing things."

"Let's look for clues," Fred said.

"Like, maybe a monster
took the snowman's things,"
said Shaggy.

Velma looked all around her.
"There are no footprints,"
she said.

Then she saw something
hanging from a tree close by.
"Jinkies," said Velma. "There's
your scarf."

Scooby found a feather and
ran toward it. "Another clue,"
he thought.

But he tripped in the big hole he
had dug earlier and rolled head
over heels halfway down the
mountain in a giant snowball.

When Scooby finally stopped rolling, he shook off the snow and could smell Scooby-Snacks. He dug another hole deeper and deeper, hoping to find them.

The gang came down the mountain to find Scooby. "Look Scooby," said Velma. "You solved the mystery." Scooby poked his head out of the snow and saw three little birds chirping loudly.

He saw the carrot, branches
and hat.

He could smell the Scooby-Snacks.

Then he saw what had
taken them.

It was not a monster.

It was a bird!

"What about our snowman?" asked Fred.

"I have an idea," said Velma.

The gang worked hard.

When they were done, Shaggy said, "Our snowman looks just like a real monster!"

"Monster!" Scooby shouted.

He dug a hole in the snow and yelled, "Scooby-Dooby-Doo!"

The End